Dear Parent,

We want to send you 8 *Dr. Seuss™ & His Friends* storybooks to encourage your child's love of reading.

As the most trusted name in learning today, we know just what that takes! Scholastic's books have been used by thousands of teachers across the country to teach millions of children to read. We're the #1 resource for parents like you for the widest variety of innovative products that help their children learn at home.

Parents turn to us to find just the right products for their children's specific needs and interests. From programs to enrich their children's skills … sensible solutions to pressing concerns … homework help, research projects, reading tips and more.

After all, we're parents, too! And, speaking as a mom, these *Dr. Seuss™ & His Friends* storybooks make story time one of the best times my family shares. My kids loves the tongue-twisting, rib-tickling antics starring Dr. Seuss's most unforgettable characters. I love the way my children's eyes light up when they hear the funny rhymes and see the hysterical illustrations. These are true classic storybooks that will be read – and enjoyed – again and again.

So, enjoy this book with your child right now. Then fill out and mail one of the order cards at left and watch your child start learning … and loving every minute of it!

Sincerely,

Mary-Alice Moore
Editorial Director
(and mother of three!)

)TE: If all of the cards are missing,
ease write to:
. Seuss™ & His Friends
Scholastic
). Box 6038
fferson City, MO 65102-6038

This book belongs to ...
©Illus. Dr. Seuss 1957

GROLIER
BOOK CLUB EDITION

Green Eggs and Ham

By Dr. Seuss

BEGINNER BOOKS
A DIVISION OF RANDOM HOUSE

 Published in New York by Beginner Books, Inc., and simultaneously in Toronto, Canada, by Random House of Canada, Limited. Library of Congress Catalog Card Number: 60-13493. Manufactured in the United States of America.

V W X 6 7 8 9

I
am Sam

I
am Sam

Sam
I am

That Sam-I-am!

That Sam-I-am!

I do not like

that Sam-I-am!

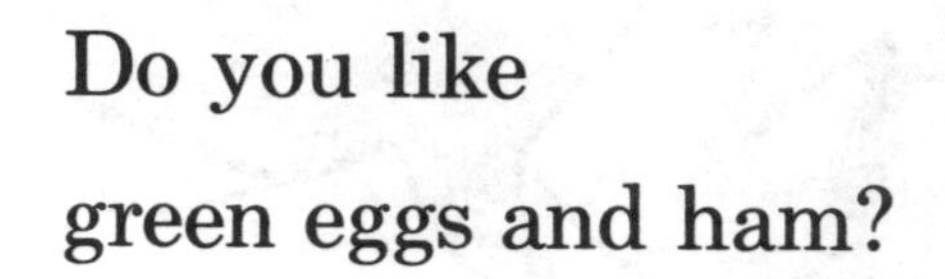

Do you like
green eggs and ham?

I do not like them,
Sam-I-am.
I do not like
green eggs and ham.

Would you like them
here or there?

I would not like them
here or there.
I would not like them
anywhere.
I do not like
green eggs and ham.
I do not like them,
Sam-I-am.

Would you like them
in a house?
Would you like them
with a mouse?

I do not like them
in a house.
I do not like them
with a mouse.
I do not like them
here or there.
I do not like them
anywhere.
I do not like green eggs and ham.
I do not like them, Sam-I-am.

Would you eat them
in a box?
Would you eat them
with a fox?

Not in a box.

Not with a fox.

Not in a house.

Not with a mouse.

I would not eat them here or there.

I would not eat them anywhere.

I would not eat green eggs and ham.

I do not like them, Sam-I-am.

Would you? Could you?

In a car?

Eat them! Eat them!

Here they are.

I would not,
could not,
in a car.

You may like them.
You will see.
You may like them
in a tree!

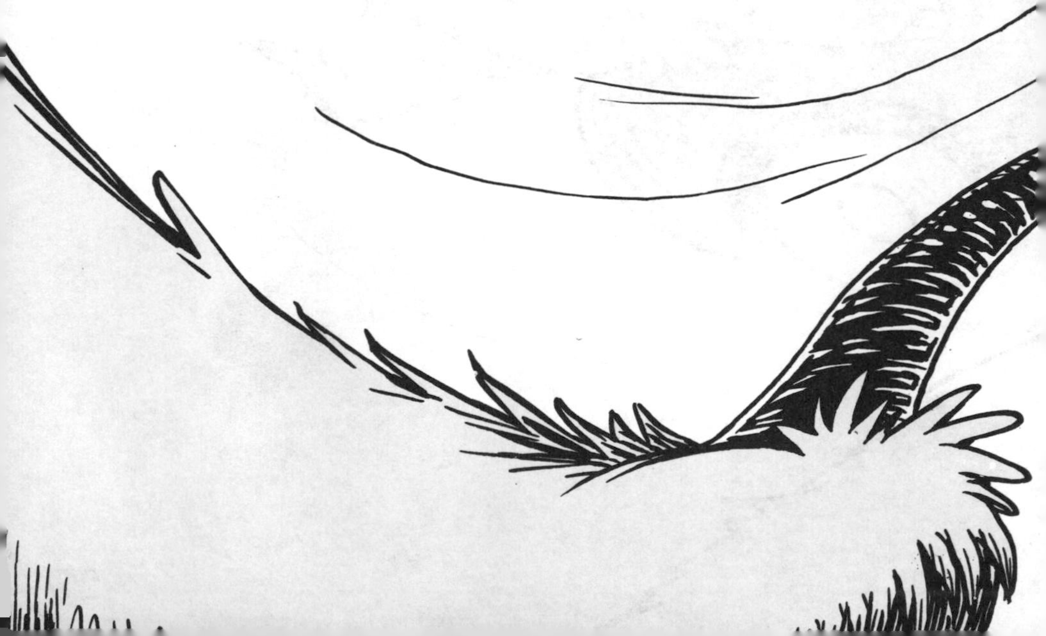

I would not, could not in a tree.
Not in a car! You let me be.

I do not like them in a box.

I do not like them with a fox.

I do not like them in a house.

I do not like them with a mouse.

I do not like them here or there.

I do not like them anywhere.

I do not like green eggs and ham.

I do not like them, Sam-I-am.

A train! A train!

A train! A train!

Could you, would you,

on a train?

Not on a train! Not in a tree!

Not in a car! Sam! Let me be!

I would not, could not, in a box.

I could not, would not, with a fox.

I will not eat them with a mouse.

I will not eat them in a house.

I will not eat them here or there.

I will not eat them anywhere.

I do not eat green eggs and ham.

I do not like them, Sam-I-am.

Say!

In the dark?

Here in the dark!

Would you, could you, in the dark?

I would not, could not,

in the dark.

Would you, could you,
in the rain?

I would not, could not, in the rain.
Not in the dark. Not on a train.
Not in a car. Not in a tree.
I do not like them, Sam, you see.
Not in a house. Not in a box.
Not with a mouse. Not with a fox.
I will not eat them here or there.
I do not like them anywhere!

You do not like
green eggs and ham?

I do not
like them,
Sam-I-am.

Could you, would you,
with a goat?

I would not,
could not,
with a goat!

Would you, could you,
on a boat?

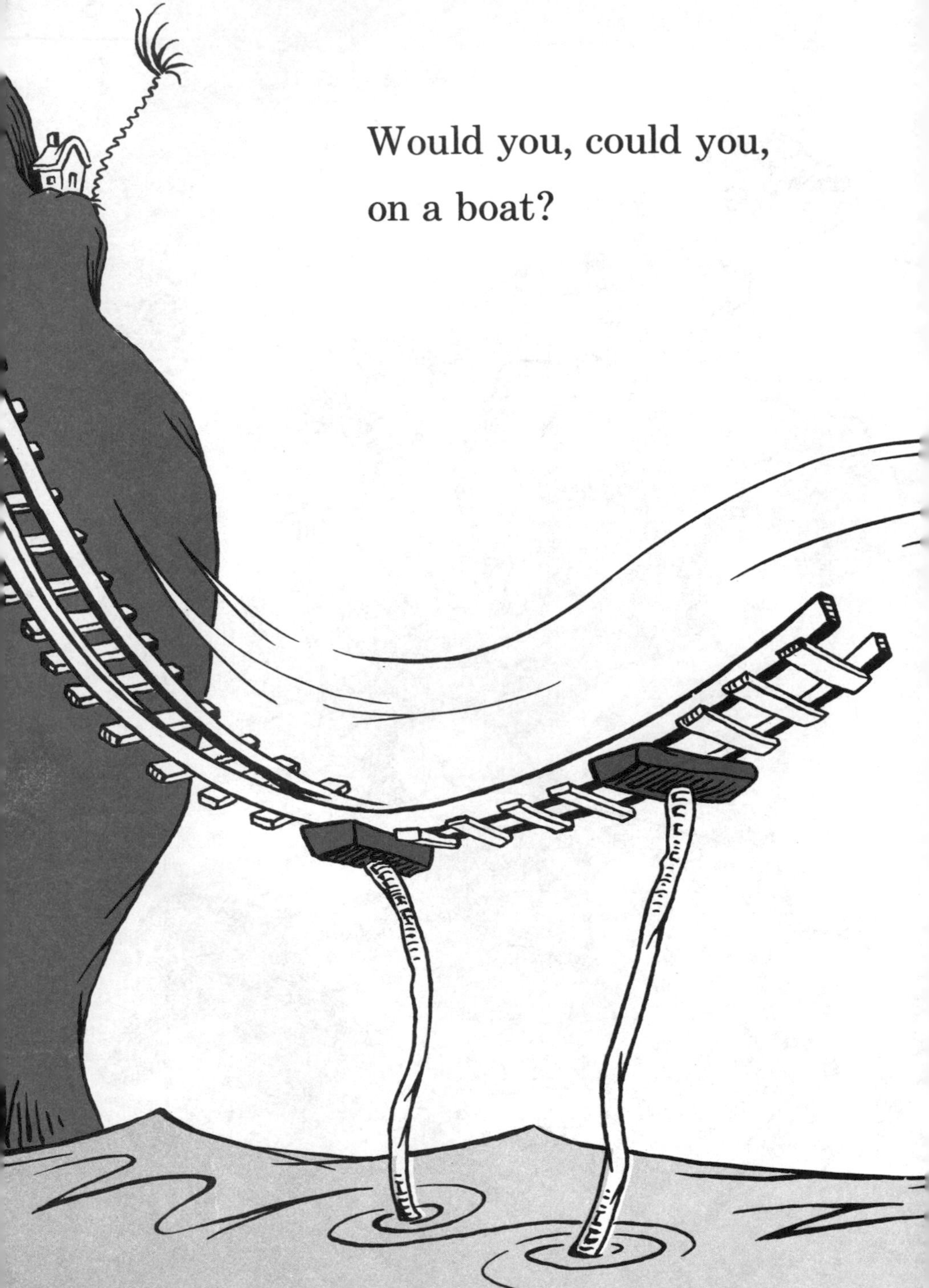

I could not, would not, on a boat.
I will not, will not, with a goat.
I will not eat them in the rain.
I will not eat them on a train.
Not in the dark! Not in a tree!
Not in a car! You let me be!
I do not like them in a box.
I do not like them with a fox.
I will not eat them in a house.
I do not like them with a mouse.
I do not like them here or there.
I do not like them ANYWHERE!

I do not like
green eggs
and ham!

I do not like them,

Sam-I-am.

You do not like them.

So you say.

Try them! Try them!

And you may.

Try them and you may, I say.

Sam!

If you will let me be,

I will try them.

You will see.

Say!

I like green eggs and ham!

I do! I like them, Sam-I-am!

And I would eat them in a boat.

And I would eat them with a goat . . .

And I will eat them in the rain.
And in the dark. And on a train.
And in a car. And in a tree.
They are so good, so good, you see!

So I will eat them in a box.

And I will eat them with a fox.

And I will eat them in a house.

And I will eat them with a mouse.

And I will eat them here and there.

Say! I will eat them ANYWHERE!

I do so like
green eggs and ham!
Thank you!
Thank you,
Sam-I-am!